D1227310

Things That Don't Make Sense

Brynn Kelly

An imprint of Enslow Publishing

WEST **44** BOOKS™

THE BAD KIDS IN 4B

Welcome to 4B

Things That Don't Make Sense

Detention Is a Lot Like Jail

Cutting Through the Noise

Please visit our website, www.west44books.com.
For a free color catalog of all our high-quality books,
call toll free 1-800-542-2595 or fax 1-877-542-2596.

Cataloging-in-Publication Data

Names: Kelly, Brynn.
Title: Things that don't make sense / Brynn Kelly.
Description: New York : West 44, 2019. | Series: The bad kids in 4B
Identifiers: ISBN 9781538382233 (pbk.) | ISBN 9781538382240 (library bound) | ISBN 9781538383124 (ebook)
Subjects: Schools--Juvenile fiction. | Families--Juvenile fiction. | Friendship--Juvenile fiction.
Classification: LCC PZ7.K455 Th 2019 | DDC [E]--dc23

First Edition

Published in 2019 by
Enslow Publishing LLC
101 West 23rd Street, Suite #240
New York, NY 10011

Copyright © 2019 Enslow Publishing LLC

Editor: Theresa Emminizer
Designer: Seth Hughes

Photo credits: Cover (background) © istockphoto.com/Peshkova; cover (person) © istockphoto.com/4x6

Printed in the United States of America

CPSIA compliance information: Batch #CS18W44: For further information contact
Enslow Publishing LLC, New York, New York at 1-800-542-2595.

THE BAD KIDS IN 4B

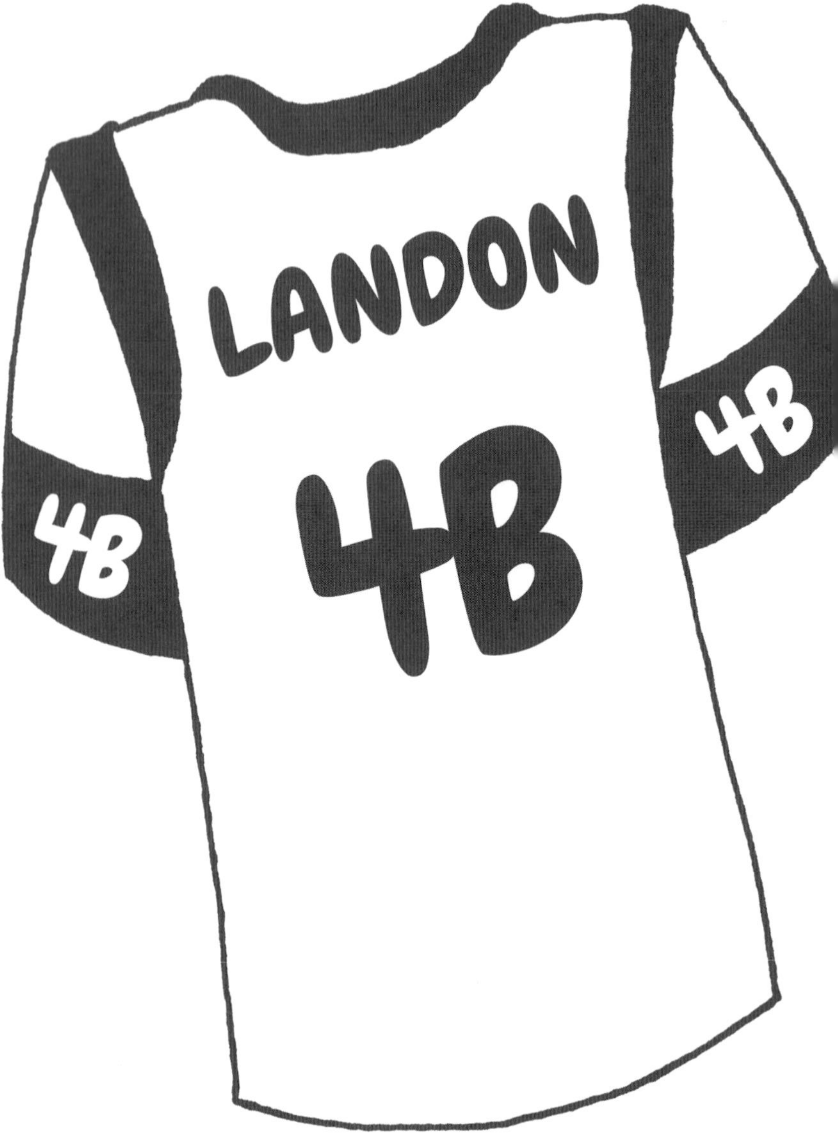
LANDON
48
48
48

DETENTION SLIP

NAME Landon Meyers

DATE November 10th

GRADE 7th

TEACHER Miss Andrews

REASON Landon skateboarded into class today. He wouldn't sit still. When I told him to pay attention, he skateboarded back out.

Chapter One
The Report Card

"Watch out!" said Landon. He jumped onto his bed. "The dragon turned the floor into lava."

Landon's little brother, Jake, jumped after him. Jake loved this game. He was six years old. He spent most of his time playing make-believe. Landon was really good at coming up with the stories. This afternoon, they were knights. They were fighting a dragon. They needed to save their town.

"I'll throw this rock at him," said Jake. He pretended to pick up a rock.

"You'll need something bigger than that."

Jake opened his arms wide. He pretended to pick up a larger rock. Landon laughed.

"Here!" Landon held his hand out. "Take this sword. On the count of three, we'll charge at him."

They stood on the bed ready to attack. Jake held up his arm.

"One, two, three!"

They jumped off the bed and ran toward a chair in the corner. Landon slashed at it. Jake stabbed it with his pretend sword.

"He's dead," said Landon. "Good job, Sir Jake!"

"Time for dinner, boys!" their mom called from downstairs.

"Race?"

They ran down the stairs into the kitchen. Landon beat Jake, who came running after. Landon sat down and grabbed his water glass. He was out of breath, but happy.

"I hate when you do that. I've told you that before, Landon. Stop acting like a little kid. You're being a bad influence on your brother. I don't need two crazy boys running around."

His mother put a plate of chicken on the table. Her blonde hair was twisted into a bun. She was wearing a skirt and a buttoned shirt. She looked like she was going out.

"I have to leave in a couple minutes. I have a parent-teacher conference at Jake's school tonight."

It's parent-teacher conference time? Landon thought. Didn't they just have conferences not too long ago? Maybe this was a special one just for Jake. Hopefully Landon's school wasn't having them. Landon had gotten in trouble last time. His parents took away his computer. He wasn't allowed to hang out with his friends for two weeks.

Jake started blowing bubbles in his milk. Their mom looked at him. He stopped for a minute. Then blew a few more.

"See, Landon? Look at what your behavior is doing to your little brother. He used to be a good kid. Now, he blows bubbles at the table. And I have to go see the teacher about how he's acting in class."

She grabbed her coat. "I have to go. Your dad will be home soon. Please be good. I don't need to come home to a mess."

She kissed Jake on the head and headed out the door. Landon heard the lock click.

"Oh no," said Jake. "I hear another dragon."

"We'd better get it!"

They pretended to chase the dragon around the house. Landon cornered it in the living room. He raised his arm. Jake jumped, his arms wide open. He fell into a side table instead, knocking it over. The lamp on the table dropped to the floor. A piece cracked off. Landon heard footsteps on the porch.

"Dad?" said Jake.

Landon went to the door to look. It was only the mailman. He unlocked the door to get the mail. There were a few bills. And one letter from his school.

Landon knew it was his report card. He also knew it would be bad news. He needed to hide it. Especially because they broke the lamp. And his mom was mad about Jake acting out more. *No*, Landon thought. *I'll just have to keep it a secret for now*. He folded the envelope. He would hide it in his room later.

"Hey, son."

Landon's dad walked up the driveway. He had on his long coat. It made him look even taller than he was. Landon thought he looked like a detective.

"Anything good?"

"Not really, just some stuff for you and mom." Landon handed him the mail. They headed inside.

"What happened here?" His dad pointed to the lamp on the floor.

"Dragons!" said Jake.

"We got a little bit carried away."

"Clean it up before your mom comes home. We don't need her yelling about it."

"I will," said Landon.

He was glad his dad didn't care. His dad wasn't someone who yelled. He wanted everyone to get along. To have a good time. He didn't like dealing with unpleasant things. Landon's mom was the one who did the yelling. She gave the punishments.

"And make sure you get your homework done. Don't need her nagging about that either." He headed into the kitchen.

Jake helped Landon with the lamp. Only a small piece had broken off. You could hardly see it. Landon turned it so the broken part faced the wall. He hoped his mom wouldn't notice.

Landon still had to hide his report card in his room. He looked to make sure no one was watching. His dad was eating dinner in the family room. Jake was building with blocks. Landon pushed the letter under his mattress. He would figure out what to do with it tomorrow. For now, it would have to stay there. He couldn't risk someone finding it.

Chapter Two
A Difficult Decision

Landon took the envelope to school the next day. His mom only worked part-time, so on her days off she drove them to school in the morning. It was nice to not have to stand outside. But sometimes Landon wished he took the bus. He kept his report card in his planner.

"Have a good day. And be good!" his mom said.

Landon walked to his locker. He took the envelope out of his bag. He didn't want anyone to see him with it. He hid behind the door as he ripped it open. Sure

enough, he had an "F" in every subject. Well, every big subject. He had a B- in gym and art. Miss Andrews had written comments at the bottom.

Landon tried to sound out the words.

"Landon is behind in all of his classes. He re-fu-ses to do his work. Many times he does not lis-ten to dire-ctions." *Refuses?* Okay, so maybe he wouldn't take a few quizzes or tests. Maybe he stared out the window instead of at the chalkboard. But "refuse" sounded harsh.

Landon felt his heart race. He was going to fail seventh grade. There was no way he would survive this. His mother would never forgive him. She would never trust him. He would never be allowed to do anything fun. She thought he was a bad kid. She thought he failed because he didn't try. That wasn't true at all.

There was a signature line at the end of the page. "Please sign and return to school with your child." A new panic filled Landon. *What am I going to do?* Miss Andrews would know his parents hadn't seen his report card. But there was no way he could give it to his mom.

"What's going on, Landon?"

Owen stood next to him. His locker was next to Landon's locker. Owen was also in 4B. The "bad kids" classroom. Landon didn't think he was a bad kid. He just had a hard time paying attention in class. He also got nervous a lot. Sometimes, it was really bad. Sometimes he just left school early because he couldn't stand it.

"Nothing, just trying to figure something out."

Owen looked over. He saw the report card in Landon's hand.

"Another great report card, huh?" Owen threw his bag in his locker. "You should do what I do. Just fake it."

"Fake my mom's name?"

"Yeah, I do it all the time. It's better than seeing my mom's face when I bring home an F. Miss Andrews has no idea."

It would be perfect if it worked, Landon thought. And it would be better than telling his mom. He decided to try.

"How do I do it?"

"You need something your mom signed. Then just hold the papers together. The light will shine through so you can see it. And you can just trace her name."

Landon searched his locker for any paper his mom had signed. There was a math test from a few weeks ago. He had gotten an "F." Miss Andrews had made

X <u>*Alicia Meyers*</u>

him take it home to sign. "Alicia Meyers" was written at the bottom in large letters. He put his report card over the page. He traced over the name. It didn't look perfect. But he thought it would pass.

"Looks good to me," said Owen. The bell rang for first period.

They were the last to get to class. Landon sat in the front. It wasn't his choice. Miss Andrews had put him there. She thought he needed the extra attention. It didn't make any difference. Landon could sit in the front or the back. He still wouldn't do any better. It wasn't his fault. Nothing made sense to him. No one understood that. His parents thought he wasn't trying. They thought he didn't care about school. School had been so easy for them. Why was he having so much trouble?

Miss Andrews pulled a chair to the front of the room. She sat down. "Landon, could you start us off this morning? We're on page 52 of our book."

Landon's face got hot. He hated reading out loud. Someone always laughed when he did. He stumbled through a paragraph. Then Katie took over.

Landon felt his chair move. It felt like someone was bouncing their foot on it. He turned to see Jordan. He was slouched in his chair. His legs were out in front of him. One foot was on the leg of Landon's chair.

"Can you not do that?"

Jordan just ignored him. He was staring out the window at nothing.

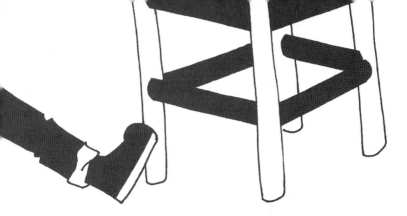

Landon got a little bit louder. "Hello? Can you stop doing that? It's annoying."

Jordan stopped tapping. He leaned forward in his chair.

"Got a problem with it? Too bad. What are you going to do about it?"

Jordan seemed older than other kids in the room. He was a lot taller and bigger. If Landon got into a fight with him, Jordan would win.

"Landon, turn around. I'm about to start our lesson. And you'll need to pay attention."

Jordan laughed under his breath. "Yeah, little Landon, pay attention."

Landon felt his body get stiff with anger. He hated Jordan. He made being in 4B even worse. There was no reason he needed to be such a jerk. They were all stuck there together. Landon felt his chair moving again. He wanted to yell at Jordan, but he didn't. It was easier to let him win.

Chapter Three
A Lunchtime Deal

Every day, Landon looked forward to lunch at 12:30. It was the one time he didn't have to think. It gave him a break from the stress of the classroom. He measured time in hours until lunch. And then hours until dismissal. It seemed like his classmates did, too.

Jordan was the most annoying right before lunch. He tapped his feet, his pencil, his fingers. Landon thought he felt the whole classroom move. Katie, another kid in 4B, refused to do any more work 10 minutes before lunch. If Miss Andrews started a new topic, she complained until Miss Andrews stopped. Some days, Miss Andrews yelled at her. Some days, she didn't bother.

"Okay, class," said Miss Andrews, "I know it's almost lunchtime. Before you go, please hand in your report cards. Remember that they need to be signed. If your parents did not sign it, I will be calling them."

Landon panicked for a minute. Was he really going to hand in his report card like this? *What other choice do I have?* he thought. If he didn't hand it in, then Miss Andrews would call his parents. They would ground him. He wouldn't be able to see his friends for a very long time. He had to hand it in. He would just act normally. Miss Andrews wouldn't think anything of it. Owen said he did it a bunch of times.

Landon pulled the card out from his book bag. He placed it on the pile on Miss Andrews' desk. He looked at the signature for a second. Hopefully, she wouldn't notice anything different. The rest of the class lined up. Mrs. Taylor walked them down to lunch. Like prisoners.

"So, you did it, huh?" said Owen. He took a seat across from Landon.

"Yeah, I almost chickened out. I thought about what would happen if Miss Andrews found out. But then I thought about what would happen if my parents found out about my grades. That'd be even worse."

Landon pulled a sandwich from his bag. It was cut perfectly from corner to corner. No crust.

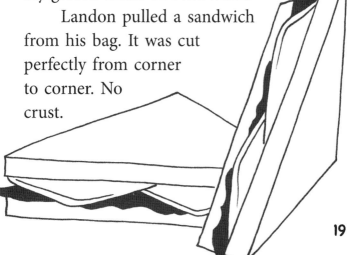

The right amount of ham and cheese. His mom was great at everything. Even at making sandwiches. His dad was great at everything, too. He had been promoted three times in five years at his company. Even Jake was good at school. His teachers said he might be able to skip first grade.

Everyone in Landon's family was perfect. Except for Landon. He wished he were smarter. His parents never had to try for anything. Life was just easy for them. Sometimes, he wondered if they had adopted him. It didn't make sense that he was their kid.

"I'm sure you'll be fine," Owen said, making a tower out of his crackers. "I've faked my mom's name like six times. I only got caught once."

"What happened when you got caught?" Landon wanted to plan for everything. Just in case.

"Miss Andrews called my mom. Then she and my dad had to come in for a meeting. And Miss Andrews called my mom after the next report card."

"What did your mom say?"

Owen looked uncomfortable. Landon didn't know much about his family. But Owen didn't look like he wanted to talk about it.

"I got in trouble," he said. He stuffed five crackers into his mouth.

I can't do anything about it now, thought Landon. He would just have to wait and see what happened.

"What are you idiots doing?" Jordan slammed his lunch tray on the table. He sat down next to Landon. Even sitting, Jordan was a foot taller than him.

"What do you want, Jordan?"

"Nothing, just wanted to check on my favorite buddy." He tousled Landon's hair.

"What's new in Loser-ville?"

Owen sat very quietly. His head was down.

"Nothing. Leave us alone," Landon said.

"Really? Seems someone here lied about his report card." Jordan stuffed chips into his mouth.

Landon turned. "You were spying on us? You're such a creep!"

"A creep? Maybe. But a creep with a price."

Owen had started grouping his fruit snacks by color. He ate them in rainbow order.

"What do you mean, a price? You aren't planning to tell, are you?" Landon whispered. He couldn't risk anyone else hearing.

"I won't tell," said Jordan. "If you give me something I want."

Landon thought for a moment.

"Fine, what do you want?"

"I want both of your ice cream coupons for Spirit Week."

Hamilton Middle School had a Spirit Week each spring. Each day of the week had a fun activity or theme. One was always ice cream day. On that day, each kid got one coupon for a free ice cream sundae. It was the one of the best days of the miserable school year.

"Okay," said Landon. "You can have our coupons."

Owen shook his head, but said nothing.

"Great," said Jordan. He started to get up. "Oh, and I want first pick of what's in your lunch.

For two weeks. I'm getting sick of this cafeteria food."

Landon didn't have a choice. Jordan had trapped him in his own lie. To back down now would ruin it.

"Fine, you can get first pick of what's in my lunch. But only for a week."

Jordan thought about it. Then he held out his hand.

"Deal." He went and sat at his usual table.

"What are you doing?" said Owen.

"Whatever I need to do to stop my parents from finding out."

Chapter Four
The Perfect Family

Owen came over on Saturday. A new video game had just come out, and Landon was dying to play it. He and Owen could spend hours playing. Landon loved games. But he loved video games the most. He wanted to make video games when he grew up. It would be the best. Just imagine getting paid to make games and play games! It was the only thing in the world Landon wanted to do. Of course, his parents didn't know that. His mom would think it was stupid. And his dad wanted him to go into business. Just like he did.

"Watch out," yelled Landon. A big alien ran toward Owen's player. He died right away.

"I suck at this game."

"Give me that." Landon grabbed the controller. He started up a new game.

There was something so perfect about video games. Landon loved the stories. And the artwork. But most of all, he loved being a hero. In a video game, Landon was good at everything. There wasn't any game he hadn't won. He dreamed of one day making a game that only he could beat.

Right now, he was on an alien planet. He had crash-landed and needed to get to his ship. A group of aliens circled him. He quickly beat them all.

"No fair! You've played this before."

"It's all about patterns," said Landon. "Watch his attack. See how he moves in threes? You have to wait for the right moment to hit him. Each enemy has a different pattern. Once you find it, you can beat him."

"I guess that makes sense."

They were sitting on the floor in Landon's bedroom. Owen leaned back against Landon's bed.

"Have you gotten any phone calls?"

Landon knew he was talking about his report card.

"No, it looks like Miss Andrews bought it. And it doesn't seem like Jordan told anyone. So, that's good."

"See, it all worked out," said Owen. "Except you lost us our ice cream coupons."

"I know, I'm sorry. I'll get you a whole box of ice cream."

"It's not the same. Oh, good hit!"

Landon had delivered a big punch to the final enemy. He fell to the ground. Landon's character got on his ship.

Landon put the controller down. "What do you think of that new girl?"

"Mila? She seems okay. I heard she screamed at Mrs. Marks until she cried."

"Have you heard why she's here?"

"No, she only really talks to Katie. Maybe her old school kicked her out? And 4B was the only place that would take her?" Owen said.

"See if you can find out more," said Landon. "You sit right in front of Katie."

"Why do you care?"

"I'm just curious." Landon started to organize the books on his desk. "I've caught her looking at me a few times."

"Curious? You like her!"

"That's not true." He looked Owen right in the eye. "I just want to make sure she's not in a gang or anything. I don't need another reason to watch my back."

"Yeah, okay." Owen didn't look convinced, but he didn't argue.

There was a knock at the door. It was Landon's mom.

"Owen's mom is here," she said. She was wearing a purple dress with high heels. "Also, my guests will be here soon. Please change into something nice, Landon."

Once a month, his mom hosted a dinner party. Couples from the neighborhood came. And some parents of kids from school. He and Jake had to dress up and greet them. *All so that Mom can show off our perfect family*, Landon thought. After an hour or so, he and Jake would go upstairs. They would eat dinner in his room. The adults ate in the dining room.

"See you later," said Owen.

Landon's brother popped his head into his room. He had on a blue button-down shirt. Red suspenders held up his pants. Landon thought Jake looked like he belonged in a commercial.

"Ready?" Jake asked.

"Not yet, I have to get my fancy clothes on. I'll meet you down there."

Landon changed and headed downstairs. There were a few people there already.

"You remember my son, Landon."

His mom grabbed his hand. She was standing in front of a man and woman he didn't remember.

"Of course!" the woman said. She had lipstick on her front teeth.

"Nice to see you again," said the man. "Your mom tells me you just made the honor roll. Congrats!"

Landon forced himself to smile. His mom always did this. She lied to everyone. She loved to pretend they were all perfect. Well, at least that Landon was perfect just like they were. The man told a joke. Landon escaped while they laughed. He found Jake sitting in a corner. He was eating a slice of cake.

"Wanna get out of here?" Landon asked.

Jake nodded, and they went upstairs.

Chapter Five
Too Stupid

The next school day started with math. Landon wondered why any teacher started the day with math. It put everyone in a bad mood. The class was loud that morning. Mila and Katie were talking. Jordan was in the back. He was throwing a paper ball against the wall. Another kid had his feet up on his desk.

"Good morning, class. We're going to get started. Please take your seats."

Miss Andrews drew two lines on the board. She wrote out $y = 2x + 3$.

"Does anyone remember what this is?"

A few students looked down at their desks.

"This is called an algebraic equation. Remember when we solved for x? Today we are going to make this into a line."

She circled the number 2.

"This is the slope of the line. Does anyone know what that means?"

"It's where the line is," Mila said.

"Almost, Mila. It's how steep the line is. Think about a mountain."

She drew two mountains on the board. One was tall. One was short.

None of this made sense to Landon. What did math have to do with mountains? How could you use numbers to make a line? This was art, not math. All of this was pointless. Even if he could learn it. Video games didn't need algebra.

Landon didn't even know how to solve for x. There was no way he could learn this stuff.

Landon looked over at Owen. He was drawing. Half his worksheet was covered in doodles.

"The other number tells us where to plot our first point. This line will cross the y-axis at 3." Miss Andrews put a dot at the 3 on the y-axis.

Landon couldn't pay attention. He was already failing. Why should he try? It didn't matter if Miss Andrews reviewed things with him. Or if Mrs. Taylor tried to help. The numbers got all mixed up in his head. He knew what they were. But they didn't make sense when he wrote them down. It was like seeing a face you forgot you knew. No amount of time could help him remember.

"Now you'll practice on your own. Please work in pairs on the sheet I gave you."

Landon moved one desk to the left to work with Owen. Miss Andrews came over to them.

"Landon, why don't you work with Mila? And Katie can work with Owen."

But he always worked with Owen. Was he being punished? He grabbed his worksheet. Mila sat in the third row. There was an empty seat next to her.

"Hey," said Mila.

"Hey," said Landon.

"Why don't you do half the problems? I'll do the other half. Then we can share answers."

Landon looked at the sheet. It was covered in little graphs. There were equations next to each one. Letters and numbers mixed together. It was like another language he couldn't speak. It also didn't help that he hadn't paid attention. He looked at the first problem, $y = x - 4$. He tried to remember what Miss Andrews said. The number 4 was important. But he didn't know why. Mila finished her work.

"Are you almost done?" She tilted her head to look. "You haven't done anything. Were you waiting for me to do it all?"

She looked angry. But Landon thought she was cute. She had two freckles on one side of her mouth. They moved when she talked.

"Hello? Earth to Landon! I'm not doing all the work."

"Sorry," he said quietly. "I don't know how to do it."

"But Miss Andrews just told us. Were you listening?"

"No," said Landon.

Mila rolled her eyes. She grabbed his paper. She explained how to do the problem. It still didn't make sense to Landon. He was getting annoyed at her. Yet another person who thought he wasn't trying. Landon looked away, getting upset.

Then Mila said, "You aren't lying, are you? You really don't understand."

Landon shook his head. He pushed his hair back. Mila looked at him.

"I'm sorry. I thought you were lying. I thought you just wanted me to do all the work. Does Miss Andrews know?"

Landon sat back in his chair.

"It doesn't matter. I'm just too stupid to understand."

"That can't be true."

"Well it is, so don't worry about it."

Landon felt bad for being cold to Mila. She didn't say anything after that.

"Let's review the answers, class," Miss Andrews said, chalk in hand. "I want everyone to participate. We have a big state test coming up in a month. You'll all need the practice to prepare."

A state test? thought Landon. This was terrible. This was one test he couldn't refuse. One more thing to worry about. He saw Owen rock in his chair. Mrs. Taylor went over to him.

Landon had failed the last state test. He had finished less than half of the questions. And most of those were probably wrong. Now he had to do that all over again. Maybe he could get out of it? He would need a note from his mom. Faking her name was one thing. It was a lot harder to fake a whole note. Maybe he could fake being sick? He wasn't a very good actor, though. It looked like he would have to take it. And he would just have to fail. Again.

Chapter Six

Truth and Lies

Landon was tired by the time he got home. He threw his book bag on the floor and fell onto the couch. A pillow dropped on his head. He never wanted to go back to school. It was so tiring. And boring. He was just done with all of it. The only good thing about school was hanging out with Owen. *And I guess Mila*, he thought. But Owen wasn't always there. And Mila probably thought he was a loser. She would never like him now. He felt something poke his arm.

"Cut it out, Jake. I had a bad day."

"But I'm hungry. Can I have a snack?" His little brother looked at him. His eyes were wide.

"Ugh!" Landon got up. He went to the fridge.

"Cheese stick?" He handed it to his brother. Jake grabbed it and ran into the living room. Landon opened one for himself. He sat down at the kitchen table.

Landon hoped that Owen was okay. He decided to give him a call. Owen sounded tired when he picked up.

"I'm feeling better," Owen said. "It was really stupid. I just started to think about last year. How hard the test was then. I don't want to take it again. But my mom won't write me an excuse."

"Yeah. We're both stuck taking tests." Landon pulled off a long, skinny string of cheese. He held it up over his mouth and ate it.

"At least you don't panic," Owen said.

"Yeah, but at least you know stuff. I might as well panic. I won't get any answers right anyway," Landon said.

"I guess so."

Landon heard footsteps outside. And then his mother's voice.

"Thank you, Miss Andrews. Yes, please call next week."

Landon felt his stomach sink. His mom must know.

"I have to go, Owen. My mom just got home. I think Miss Andrews told her."

"Oh, man. Sorry about that. I guess your handwriting isn't that good after all. I'll talk to you later. Unless you're grounded forever."

"Thanks. You're so helpful."

Landon heard a key in the lock. He tried to run upstairs. But his mom came

through the
door before he
could escape. She
did not look happy.

"Landon James,
you stop right there.
Guess who I was just
talking to?"

Landon turned
around. He couldn't look
at his mom. He felt too
embarrassed. He didn't reply.

"Your teacher, Miss
Andrews." His mom dropped her
bags on the counter. She took off her heels.

"She thought it was weird I hadn't
called her. She said I always call when your
grades are low. And your report card had
been so bad. She was surprised I signed
it without calling. It was strange. So, she
decided to touch base with me."

Landon was frozen. His arms and legs wouldn't move. His mouth felt very dry. He was worried he might be stuck like that. Maybe this is how Owen felt when he panicked. He couldn't control his body. He closed his eyes tight. Maybe this was a bad dream.

"Don't you ignore me, Landon!" His mom came closer. "Landon!"

Her voice broke the spell. He could move again. Though he wasn't sure what to say. "I'm sorry" didn't seem like enough. He couldn't defend what he did. His mom wouldn't understand. She would think he was lying. That he was being lazy and trying to hide it. He sat down at the table.

"I can't believe you would do this. That you would lie like this. Forging my signature on your report card. What will your father think? What must Miss Andrews think?"

His mom always cared what people thought. Landon didn't think his dad would care. He thought Landon would grow out of this. That his grades were low because he was a teenager. And Miss Andrews was a teacher. She had seen worse students than him. Landon watched his mom fill a pot with water. She banged it onto the stove.

"We give you everything. Everything you could ever want. And you do this? What else can a mother do?"

She dumped a jar of sauce into another pot. Then slammed that onto the stove, too. *How long is she going to go on?* Landon wondered. Could this get any worse? He watched her bang a few more things onto the counter. She was quiet. Landon thought she might be done. But his dad got home a minute later.

"Guess what your son did?" asked his mom.

Mom always called Landon his dad's son when something bad happened. His dad looked confused.

"He faked my name on his report card. And he's failing everything."

"Not everything. I'm passing gym and art."

His mom laughed. "Great, so you can be a gym teacher. Or a homeless artist."

The pot started to boil over. She lowered the heat. Landon's dad took his shoes off.

"Calm down, Alicia. The boy will be fine."

"Fine? How will he get into college? Or ever get a job? You have to start trying, Landon. You can't skate by forever."

"I do try." Landon could feel his face get hot.

"Don't lie to me," his mother said. She mixed the pasta. "Miss Andrews told me your grades. They would get better if you tried. Just a little bit."

Landon needed to leave. He couldn't stand being home right now. He grabbed his skateboard.

"Where are you going?" His mom followed him outside.

"Landon!"

He took off down the street.

Chapter Seven
A New Plan

Landon skateboarded as fast as he could.
He avoided the slush and dirt-flecked
snow left over from a too-early storm.
The November air felt good on his face.
It helped cool him down. He wasn't sure
where he was going. But he didn't want to
be home. How could his mom not listen
to him? It didn't matter what he said. She
would never trust him. There was no point
in trying. Maybe it would be better to
pretend he was lazy. That he was failing on
purpose. Being honest wasn't helping.

"Hey, Landon!"

A voice called as he passed. He stopped. Mila was getting mail from a mailbox. She walked over to him.

"What are you doing?"

"Just out skateboarding." He was out of breath. He had been going faster than he thought.

"Where are you going?" she asked.

"Nowhere, really." A car came down the street. They moved onto the sidewalk.

"Is everything okay?" Mila asked.

"Everything's fine."

"Okay." She looked at him. "Do you want to come over?"

Landon thought about his parents. They were so mad at him right now. They would be angrier if he went to Mila's house. "Sure," Landon said.

Mila led the way up the driveway. She opened the door and let Landon in. The house was small, but nice.

"My aunt is still at work. She'll be home in a half hour."

A big, gray cat jumped onto the table.

"Beau, behave yourself!" Mila put the cat back on the floor. "Make yourself at home. Do you want something to drink?"

"Yeah, water would be great."

Landon leaned his skateboard against the wall. He sat down on the couch. Mila brought his glass over. She sat down next to him. She was pretty close. She smelled like vanilla.

"Why are parents so difficult?" Landon asked.

"I don't know. Mine aren't great. That's why I'm here," Mila said.

Landon remembered Mila talking about her mom. She was in treatment for something. He felt bad for complaining.

"I didn't mean to…I'm sorry." Landon moved in his seat.

"I know. It's okay. You can still have annoying parents," Mila said.

Landon smiled. Then said, "My mom found out my grades. Miss Andrews called her. I'm failing everything."

Mila took a sip of her water. "That really stinks."

"Yeah, and it gets worse. I faked my mom's name on my report card. I didn't want her to know. Owen said he does it all the time. But now my mom knows my grades. And she knows I faked her name. I can't go home. Not for a while."

"We have ice cream," Mila says.

"What?"

"We have ice cream if you want some. My aunt eats it when she's upset. She says it helps."

"Do you think it helps?"

"A little."

"What kind do you have?"

Mila got up to check the freezer.

"Chocolate or… just chocolate."

She came back with a tub of ice cream. She handed it to him. He looked at it. There was only one spoon.

"We can share. Fewer dishes."

He took a bite and put the spoon back in. She picked it up and did the same.

"So, what happened when your mom found out?" Mila asked.

"She started yelling that I don't try. That I'll never get into college. Or have a job. Usual stuff."

"Does she know you do try?"

"She thinks I'm lying if I say that. *If you tried, you wouldn't fail.* She always says that," Landon said.

The front door opened. Mila jumped up.

"Aunt Julie, this is Landon. He's from my class."

Her aunt looked young. She was carrying a lot of bags. "Nice to meet you."

"I can help with that," Landon said.

Mila grabbed a few bags. She helped her aunt put away the groceries. Landon liked Mila's house. It was smaller than his. It was a bit messier, too. But it was comfortable. He felt welcome.

"I'll be working in the back. Let me know if you want me to start dinner."

Her aunt left them. Mila sat back down next to Landon.

"So, what happens when you do try?"

"What do you mean?"

"What happens when you try in class?"

"It's hard to explain. It's like another language. Like Miss Andrews is saying things I kind of understand. I get every other word. But I don't get the whole thing. And with numbers, it's even worse."

"What if I tried to teach you? Or Owen? We could come over tomorrow. We could bring our books and review everything."

"I don't think it would help."

"But it couldn't hurt." Mila smiled. Her eyes lit up. She looked so cute. It was hard to say no to her.

"Okay, but it would have to be right after school. And you couldn't stay long. My mom is working tomorrow. But she'll be home around 4:40. I'm sure I'll be grounded. She'll be mad if she sees you"

"That's fine. We won't stay long."

"Sounds good." Landon got up. "I have to go. I'll see you tomorrow."

He skateboarded back down the street. It was getting dark. His mom would be so mad at him. Landon didn't care. He would take whatever punishment she gave.

The house was quiet when he got home. He found his mom sitting in the living room. She was reading. She looked up when he walked in. She looked mad, but also kind of relieved.

"Where were you? I called all your friends. You weren't there."

"I was at Mila's house. She's a new student."

"You could have been dead. I had no idea where you were." She closed the book on her lap. "You're grounded. Two weeks. No phone, no computer,

no friends. Now, go do your homework. If you're hungry, there's pasta in the fridge."

Landon was glad she didn't yell. He was annoyed to be grounded. He did lie about

signing her name. But he hadn't lied about trying in school.

Chapter Eight

4B Tutor Team

Mila met Landon at his locker the next afternoon. Her arms were full of books. Her bag was falling off her shoulder.

"Have enough stuff?" Landon asked.

"I think so. I just wanted to make sure I have everything we might need."

"It looks like you have more than that. Want me to take anything?"

"Sure." She shoved the pile of books into his chest.

Owen walked over with Katie. His bag was in his hands.

"We're coming over, too. If that's okay with you."

"Yeah, as long as you're gone in time."

The four of them walked the 15 minutes to Landon's house. Mila set her books on the kitchen table. She opened a few.

"Do you have paper and pencils? I brought my notebook. But I don't want to use all the paper."

Landon found some. They all sat down. The table was covered in books and paper. There were two different math books open. Everything looked very confusing. And too much to understand. *This was a stupid idea*, Landon thought. *How are they going to help me?*

"I know it looks like a lot," said Mila. "But I have a few ideas. First rule, stop me if I don't make sense."

She started with algebra. She wrote a couple of equations on the paper. They looked familiar to Landon. Mila reviewed how to solve for x. She asked Landon to try. He wasn't sure what to do.

"Think of a video game," said Owen. "Math is like a pattern in a game. Watch what Mila does. Then do the same thing. It looks different. But don't get confused by that. You solve it the same way."

Landon tried another equation. He was almost able to finish it. Mila showed him again. All four of them practiced together. Landon felt like maybe he could get better at it. Maybe things weren't so hopeless. It felt nice to have friends who wanted to help.

By the third problem, he got it right.

"Great, now on to graphs."

Mila drew a graph on her paper. She explained each part of it. She reviewed how the equation related to the graph. Landon tried to remember it all. He heard her words. But it didn't exactly make sense.

"Why don't we take a break," said Katie. "I'm hungry."

"I'll see if we have anything to eat," said Landon.

Landon started to get up. But he heard the side door open. His mom was home early. There was nothing he could do. He didn't have enough time to hide his friends. His mom stood looking at them. Her eyes were wide.

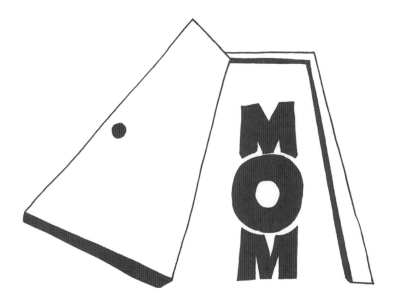

"Why are there people here?"

"Mom, I know how this looks, but–"

"But, nothing. You're grounded. And now I come home to a party? Honestly, Landon, how can I ever trust you?"

"Mrs. Meyers, it's not his fault," Mila said, standing up. "We're not having a party. We're here to help Landon."

Landon's mom looked confused.

"They're helping me study," he said.

"It's true," said Katie. "Landon is terrible at math. He doesn't get anything. We're trying to help him study for the state test. Or else he'll totally fail."

"Oh, *thanks*, Katie," said Landon. "But it is true. I've tried to tell you, Mom. I just don't understand. Miss Andrews talks, and I just don't get it. It's like another language."

Mrs. Meyers walked over to the kitchen table. She picked up a worksheet.

"Is this yours?"

Landon nodded.

"It needs a lot of work. I see what you mean. Does Miss Andrews know what's going on?"

"Not exactly. She thinks I don't try. She doesn't know why." His voice almost broke. Landon's mom looked sad.

"I didn't realize," she said. Her eyes were teary. She touched his shoulder. "I'm so sorry, Landon. I'll call Miss Andrews tomorrow. Maybe you can stay after school with her sometime this week."

"Wait," said Landon. "I want to try on my own first. Can my friends stay and keep tutoring me?"

His mom didn't look like she liked the idea. But she agreed.

"Okay, I won't call yet. They can stay, as long as you study. But you're still grounded. You did lie about signing my name."

Chapter Nine
Test Day

Landon was still nervous about the test. His friends had studied six times with him. But he still wasn't always getting the right answers. A lot of the time, he just guessed. And his reading skills still weren't very good. But it was test day. He would have to try his best. There was no more time to get ready.

"Settle down, class," Miss Andrews said. She walked around and handed out pencils. "Mrs. Taylor is going to hand out the tests. Please do not open them. I will tell you when it's time to start. You will only have three hours to finish the test. When you are done, please sit quietly. We have to wait for everyone to finish."

Katie's hand went up. "What if we have to use the bathroom?"

"Use it right now. Or wait until you are done. You can't leave the room until you're finished with the test."

This is so serious, Landon thought. It was stupid. But it also made him nervous. Owen was taking the test in another room. He didn't even have his friend there to help him feel better. He turned to look at Mila. She smiled and gave a thumbs-up.

"Okay, class. You may now begin. Remember, you can't leave until you are finished. Let me know if you have any questions."

Landon opened his test. The first section was mostly word problems. These weren't so hard. There were a few about putting things in order. Another about selling oranges. Things were going pretty well.

The next section was trickier. It was a lot of fractions. One question asked to solve an equation with fractions. Landon didn't understand fractions very well. He tried to remember what Mila had told him. He drew them out in pies. It didn't help very much. He decided to guess the answer.

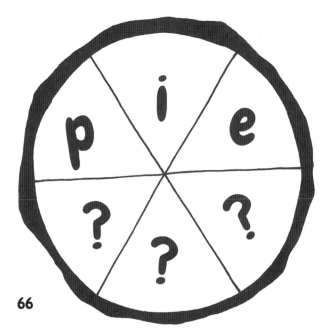

"This is so stupid!" Jordan threw down his pencil. It bounced and hit Landon's foot. "I don't want to do this."

Mrs. Taylor came over to him. "Just try your best."

"No, forget this. I want to leave." Jordan started to get up.

"Okay, Jordan. Are you finished? I can take your test if you're finished. Then you can just sit quietly."

He nodded and handed the booklet to her.

Only one question was about graphs. After all that work! Landon was able to figure it out. At least he thought he did. The last part of the test was the hardest. The test book gave three problems. Landon had to explain in words how to solve each one. It was one thing to do the solving. It was another to explain how to do it. Landon decided to just solve the problem.

He showed his work. Hopefully, that counted for something.

"Time is up, everyone. Please put your pencils down. We'll come and collect your papers."

They all talked about the test during lunch. Landon didn't feel great about it. Everyone had answers he didn't. He was sure he had failed again. Maybe his mom was right. Maybe he didn't try enough.

"Don't be so hard on yourself." Mila put her hand on his arm. "You only just started studying. That's a lot to learn in a few weeks. This won't hurt your grades. And you'll get to try again next year."

"That's not the point," Landon said, putting his head on the table. "I thought I could do it. I thought trying would help. But it didn't. I'm still just stupid."

"That's not true," said Owen. "You just learn differently."

His friends made him feel a bit better. But they still didn't solve his problem.

Landon told his mom about the test when he got home. She wasn't happy, but she didn't get mad. She told him he should talk to Miss Andrews. Maybe she could help him. Landon wasn't so sure. But maybe now there was nothing to lose.

Chapter Ten
Getting Help

Landon woke up early the next day. He wanted to get to school before anyone else. He needed to talk to Miss Andrews alone. His mom drove him into school. She had been a lot nicer since they talked. She still wasn't happy with what Landon did. But she didn't make everything seem like his fault. It would take time to get used to their new relationship. The idea that Landon needed extra help was still new to her. He might never be that perfect Honor Roll kid.

The classroom was empty when he walked in. Miss Andrews was at her desk. She was grading papers. Landon was nervous to walk in. But he knew Miss Andrews was his last chance to get help.

"You're here early," she said.

"Yeah." Landon stood for a moment with his hands in his pockets. "Miss Andrews, I need to talk."

She put her red pen down. "Have a seat. What's on your mind?"

He wanted to talk about the test. But he also remembered the signature. He should probably say sorry for that first.

"I'm sorry I faked my mom's name on my report card. I was afraid of what would happen if she found out. She's always so upset when I don't do well in school. Of course, she was more upset after she found out I lied about it."

"I did think the name looked weird. The writing was too small. And it was very strange she hadn't called. Your mom always calls if you have a failing grade. Thank you for your apology."

"I also have a favor to ask."

"Yes?"

Landon didn't know what to say. He hated asking for help. It made him feel helpless. But his friends had already tried to help. And Landon still wasn't doing any better. Miss Andrews was the last person who could help. He would just have to ask her.

"I know I did really bad on the state test. I tried, but it didn't matter. Everything is just so confusing. I can't understand any of it."

"That sounds pretty serious. Why didn't you say something before?"

Landon shrugged. "I didn't think it would matter. I thought I was too stupid to learn."

Miss Andrews looked upset. She leaned in closer and looked him in the eye.

"There is no such thing. You are not stupid. We just haven't figured out what help you need. And that is my fault. I'm the teacher. It's my job to make sure you learn. Please don't think you are stupid ever again."

Her words made Landon feel better.

"Why don't you meet with me after school? Let's say three times a week? We can review everything. You can tell me what you don't get. And it might help to talk to another student. See how they learn things."

"Actually, I've already met with a few. Mila, Owen, and Katie tried to teach me before the test. But it didn't work out too well," Landon said.

"See, you are already smarter than you think. That was a good plan. But I think this one will be even more helpful. How does it sound to you?"

"Good. It'll be nice to not be so confused. It gets tiring."

"I bet it does. Hopefully, it will get better soon. And then we can work on raising your grades a bit."

She smiled. Landon smiled back. It was the answer he had hoped for. He didn't feel so stupid anymore.

A few classmates came in. They sat down in their seats. Landon got up and sat at his desk. Miss Andrews wrote a few things on the board. Mila came through the door. Her hair was curled. She smiled at Landon. And handed him a note. He opened it and saw seven numbers written on it. She had given him her phone number. *This year isn't so bad after all*, he thought.

Want to Keep Reading?

Turn the page for a sneak peek at
the next book in the series.

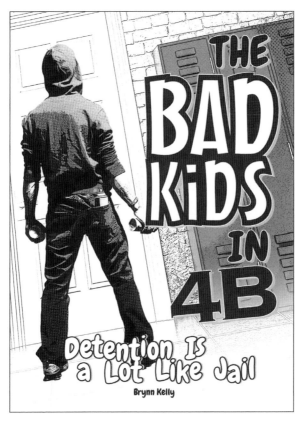

9781538382257

Chapter One
Another Terrible Day

Jordan's third alarm went off. He picked up his clock and threw it across the room. It hit the wall hard and fell. Then things were quiet again. Jordan thought about staying home. He didn't want to go to school. He never wanted to go to school. But his mom would be upset if he skipped again. He had already skipped twice this week. And he didn't want to upset his mom even more. He didn't want to listen to her yell at him. It was better to get up. He would skip a couple periods when he got there. No need to stay in class the whole day.

Jordan went into the kitchen. His mom wasn't up yet. Normally, she was out the door by this time. But not since his dad went away. Now she woke up later than Jordan. And she didn't always get to work on time.

He poured a bowl of cereal. He could hear his mom moving in her bedroom. He heard her start to cry. Jordan didn't know what to do. She had been like this for four months. Four months ago, his dad had been taken to jail. And Jordan didn't know why. He tried to ask his mom. But she never told him. She would cry when he asked her.

"I'm leaving, Mom," Jordan called to her.

"Okay, honey," she called. Her nose sounded stuffy. "I'll see you later."

Jordan got to school a few minutes late. The bell had already rung. The hallways were empty. He hated school so much. It was like a prison. He didn't understand why people came back every day. *You don't need school to be successful*, he thought. *My dad did just fine. And he didn't even graduate.*

Before he went to jail, Jordan's dad was a welder at a factory. He was pretty good. He planned to work up to head welder one day. Maybe start his own business. Jordan couldn't wait until he was 16. He planned to drop out and work. Just like his dad. He only had a few more years to wait.

ABOUT THE AUTHOR

Brynn Kelly is a writer from Buffalo, New York, where she studied English and creative writing and received a master's degree in social work. She is the author of three educational books, *The People and Culture of Venezuela*, *The Layers of Earth's Atmosphere*, and *Air Pressure and Wind*. In her free time, she enjoys doing yoga and spending time with her dog, Neno.

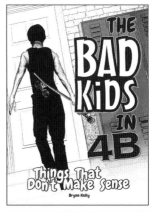

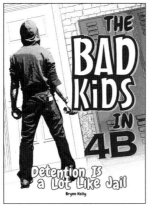

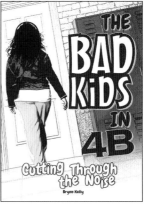

Check out more books at:

www.west44books.com

An imprint of Enslow Publishing

WEST **44** BOOKS™